This book belongs to

_____

Autumn
Publishing

Published in 2018
by Autumn Publishing
Cottage Farm
Sywell
NN6 0BJ
www.igloobooks.com

© 2018 MARVEL

LEO002 1118
2 4 6 8 10 9 7 5 3 1
ISBN 978-1-78905-616-7

Printed and manufactured in China

THE STORY OF SPIDER-MAN

Autumn
Publishing

Peter Parker was just your average teenager from Queens, New York. He lived with his Aunt May and Uncle Ben, and he attended Midtown High School. Peter was very studious and was considered one of the smartest kids in school. Unfortunately, his good grades didn't make him very popular with some of his classmates.

Flash Thompson, the school bully, regularly tormented Peter.
One day, Flash pushed him to the ground and Peter's books and
papers scattered everywhere. "Hey, Parker, you dropped your books,"
Flash sneered.

School was tough for Peter, but he was always happy at home.
Aunt May and Uncle Ben loved Peter completely. Uncle Ben
always reminded Peter that he was going to do something special
with his life.

"You are incredibly smart, Peter," Aunt May said. "You have the ability to be anything you want to be."

"Well, actually, I was thinking that I might want to be a scientist some day," Peter replied.

Uncle Ben put his arm round Peter. "Being a scientist is a very important job. Science is power. And remember – with great power comes great responsibility."

Then, one day Peter's life changed while he was on a school trip to the Science Hall. He was excited to see real-life scientists at work. But while Peter looked around at the exhibits, a spider passed through radioactive waves. Peter was so distracted, he didn't even notice the radioactive spider head right towards him.

At that moment, the
radioactive spider bit Peter!
He could never have imagined
what an impact this one bite
would have on his life. Peter
Parker would never be the same.

Before Peter knew it, he had adopted many characteristics of a spider. He could cling to walls, he was superstrong and he also had spider-sense. This meant that Peter experienced a strong tingling feeling that alerted him to danger. These skills made Peter extremely powerful.

Peter wanted to keep his identity a secret, so he stayed up all night creating a spider-suit and mask. He even stitched a large spider on the front of it.

Peter also worked hard to figure out how to control his new powers. Using his vast knowledge of science, he made web-shooters and practised shooting them in his bedroom. Peter's superstrong webs stuck to every surface. Soon, his entire room was covered in webs!

Okay, so it's not as easy as it looks, Peter thought.

Like all teenagers, Peter wanted to make money. He needed a job where he could use his powers to his advantage. So, Peter became a wrestler.

"Please welcome to the ring... Spider-Man!" the announcer would boom.

Peter used his powers to defeat every opponent. One night, Peter noticed the wrestling gym was being robbed. Peter didn't care and the robber ended up getting away.

When Peter got home later that night, he saw police cars in front of his house. He raced inside and found out that someone had attacked and hurt Uncle Ben. Aunt May and Peter were devastated.

The police officers told Peter not to worry because they had the criminal cornered at an old warehouse. But Peter knew he had to take matters into his own hands.

Peter put on his Spider-Man suit and swung through the city. He was determined to avenge Uncle Ben.

At last, Peter arrived at the warehouse. The thief was stunned as he watched Spider-Man in action. Spider-Man shot a web and trapped the criminal. After getting a good look at him, Spider-Man realised that it was the same criminal he had watched escape from the wrestling gym.

If only I had stopped him then! he thought. Peter vowed that from then on he would help others whenever it was in his power. He would never let anything like this happen again!

Just one month earlier, Peter would have been busy studying for his chemistry exam like any normal teenager, but everything had changed. He might still have to do homework from time to time, but Peter was also Spider-Man.

The next day at school, everyone couldn't stop talking about Spider-Man.

"I think he's great," Flash said, as he looked at an article about the new hero. "He's just trying to help the city."

Peter smiled. If only Flash knew who Peter really was!

The next day, Spider-Man heard about another criminal

on the loose in Manhattan. Spider-Man swung down to

confront the villain, who he discovered had the ability to control

electricity. It was Electro! The hero used his web-shooters,

and after a few tries, the Super Villain was defeated.

In that moment, Spider-Man realised something. It was his destiny

to always protect others and if he worked hard enough, maybe one

day, he could become a great Super Hero.

Spider-Man thought back to the words that Uncle Ben

always used to say: With great power comes great responsibility.

Peter Parker might seem
like your normal teenager,
but there is a part of him that
is extremely special. He is a
Super Hero who can scale
buildings and spin webs.
He is the Amazing
Spider-Man!

THE END